PREFACE

Life was different back in the early 1900's. Farmers outnumbered city folk by large numbers. The horse provided the power to operate farm machinery. There were no short workdays. On the contrary, summer work started with the rising sun and ended with evening darkness - seven days a week, 365 days a year. Oh, yes, there was a strong work ethic. Strong-minded fathers would tolerate no less.

Wow! How could people live that way? Frankly, there was no other way. We just did it. We didn't feel we were being abused, for that's the way my father, and his father before him, lived as far back as anyone could recall.

Were we jealous of the town kids back then? Not really. We had all of life's needs. In fact, town kids envied the farmer's life.

In the 1920's, the miracle of radio brought wonders — music and news — like city folks enjoyed: a minor distraction, but so marvelous.

After 4 score years, I still look back on those early days with longing. I am thankful I learned how to work and still start my workday at sunrise - if people will only let me.

DEDICATION

To my grandchildren, Nicholas 3, and Zachary 5, and all little children like them, who would like to know how rewarding it is to work.

CONTENTS

Published by

GEORGIE - FARM BOY OF THE PRAIRIE

"Hey in there! Can't anybody hear me, for cryin' out loud! It's colder than ice out here, for cat's sakes. Let me in!"

UP WITH THE BIRDS

A long time back, 80 years ago, I was a very lucky boy to be born on a Dakota prairie farm with all kinds of wonderful animals to keep me company through the years of my childhood. Here's how it was.

I'm Georgie, baby of my family - the littlest, ya know, so big brothers and sisters are always around to teach me how to do things. But, sometimes they are a big "pain in the neck" so I have to outsmart the whole bunch of 'em.

"Georgie, don't do this!" "Don't' do that!" "Hey shrimp, you're in the way!" "Go tell your Ma she wants ya." I get all kinds of guff like that.

But anyway, I ignore them and have the best life a little boy could ever want.

Even though I'm sorta small, at 6 years, I get up when Pa and the big boys bang the door on their way out to the barn - even now in winter. I have Ma help me on with my coat and cap, tie the scarf around my neck, see that my boots are buckled, then dash out to get some of all those chores done. Bein' it's so dark and snowy, I have to follow the rope Pa tied between the house and barn. He did that so no one'd get lost and wind up freezin' to death.

The barn door is froze so tight I can't get it open. I pound and pound my darn fool head off so they hear my distress calls and save me from the bitter cold - probably 50 below or more. I'm sure they hear me alright. They just ignore me. "Horse feathers," I say.

2

Finally, big Irvin lets me in, but not before properly insulting me. "Oh," he says, "it's only you." I would smash him, if I was bigger.

Ah, the barn's toasty warm. The animals give off lots of heat. Even the cracks in the wall get filled with frost, keeping the wind out.

How nice it is. The air's full of smells of wild prairie hay the men push down from the haymow, and dust from the ground feed floatin' in the air as Bob throws a measure to each cow. All this mixed with the smell of fresh cow poo tells a fella he's in a very secure place.

Ma and Pa, my brothers, and sis, Sophia, all busy themselves milkin'. Soon I'll grow enough to do that too, but for now I have the important job of feeding the calves and such.

"Git to work, Puddin Head," Pa says. He gives me the silliest nicknames.

So I take the calf pail to brother, Gordo, for milk and feed those little hungry critters who haven't learned to drink from a pail yet. It isn't easy, I tell ya, but sucking is natural for them. They nearly swallow my hand, as I hold it down in the milk. When they get a bit older they'll be able to drink on their own. Thinkin' about it, they do a lot better than people do. We've got to be around about a year before we can even talk or walk.

Well, with that big job done, I go draw some pictures with my fingernails in the thick frost on the windows. The older boys always add some crude touches. They disgust me, those rascals!

Finally, with all that done, I have time to go over and lay in the hay ahead of the horse stalls and play with the kitties. They've had their fill of milk--ready for another catnap. Hmmm. I like to hear their tiny purring motors run. That's always fun.

Morning chores done, I gotta go! Everybody's already left without me, for cryin' out loud!

Time to hightail it to the house for one of Ma's yummy breakfasts. I'm hungry as a horse for cat sakes.

Well, that's the way it is every day on the prairie farm - lot's of work, but then, lots of fun, too.

AFRAID THAT ROOSTER'S GONNA GET ME

In the wintertime the chickens keep nice and warm in the chicken house. All those egg-layin' hens give off heat like cows and horses. They're smaller, of course, but there are hundreds more of 'em.

I'm expected to help Ma gather eggs every day. Of course, being smaller, I have little accidents and break a few here and there. With my legs being rather short, it's a lot easier to get tangled up on things, ya know. Ma is very patient with me, though. She teases me in fun. "Georgie, set the eggs down first if you're going to fall, my boy." Mom is an angel - always happy and understanding and easy goin'.

My bucket holds about a dozen eggs, I'm sure. Of course, big people carry big buckets that hold probably fifty, or so. But for my size, I do pretty good.

We have mostly hens. They lay the eggs. But there are some roosters, too. Man, are those big kings of the roost scary to me. I have a lot of respect for those cocky rascals. I figure we have more than we need, but I guess those big guys are necessary to keep all those chickens in line layin' eggs.

In the summertime, it's a different story. The chickens can roam all over the farm - in the barns, in the woods, and wherever they want to go. It seems as though they get their just reward for being so generous laying lots of eggs in the wintertime.

I told ya, I have lots of respect for those roosters. Amongst other things, they have the responsibility of waking the family up every morning too. They crow their heads off sometimes. Well, I think they know I'm afraid of 'em, so I stay out of their way.

This time I let my guard down and stumble my way in between the two big silos back of the barn. I suppose you can imagine what's comin'. Sure enough, around the corner pops the big "king of the roost." Holy cow, I'm scared ta death! I stand about as tall as I know how, and yet that big bird comes up, raises his head, and stares at me, eye-to-eye. He ruffles his feathers and I fear I'm in for a terrible whompin'! Then he flies up, pops me with his feet and knocks me down. Of course, I scream like a hurt pig!

To add insult to injury, I glance around the corner and see big brothers, Irvin and Gordo, laughin' like lunatic's. Finally they realize I'm in deep trouble and save me - the big heroes!

DICK THE WONDER HORSE

Everything on our farm is run by horses . . . everything! We have many of these great animals; some big, muscular fellows to do heavy work like pulling the plows, planting corn and grain; smaller and lighter horses to do other things like pulling the sleds and buggies and such. But our farm is a dairy farm. We not only milk the cows, but also put milk in bottles and deliver it in town to stores and houses.

I'm proudest of Dick - the Wonder Horse we call him. Dick's about 18 hands, so Pa says; that's about 6 feet tall at the shoulders, I guess. Well, I'm only about two and a half feet tall, so you see, I can walk under the horse's belly - if I trust he won't kick, of course.

Dick's a buckskin color - sorta golden. He's a beauty! The boys say he was a racehorse once, and it's pretty obvious that with those long legs he must've been a winner.

Everybody loves Dick as he makes his rounds in the town each day. Not only is he a beaut to look at, but, he has a keen memory that douses cold water on the idea that animals are dumb.

Let me tell you about it.

Each morning the milk wagon, our high-wheeled buggy with top and sides, is filled with milk bottles for the milk route. I'm finally strong enough that I can handle a carrier with 6 bottles. I feel important when I bring milk down the back alleys to our customers and leave the right amount of bottles and put 'em in the iceboxes usually kept in back porches.

With two of us on each route, it's a great savings of time when we can walk down to the end of the block and have the rig waiting for us. You probably guessed it, Dick knows the whole route by heart.

"Giddy up, Dick!" He moves on, turns and goes up a block or two to the right spot every day. Folks love our great horse. Even the birds chirp happily when the giant buckskin appears each cold winter's morning, and they're rewarded with some unused oats he passes on generously. Dick, the wonder horse, is a living legend who will live on in the memory of the town folks for years to come.

Another fun horse I have is Old Dan, the Swayback. Talk about a contrast to Dick, Dan is

something else. His back is like a hammock. I've got short legs for sure, but if I run fast I can jump up on Dan's low slung back with ease. I always pretend I'm in a circus when I ride Dan. After jumping on him, I stand on his rump, bouncing up and down like a jumping jack as he trots around the yard.

Ma has a tizzy worryin' about me. "Georgie, my boy, don't fall," she yells. "You'll hurt yourself." I only laugh. "Ha, ha." (Mothers get so carried away.)

"Ha, ha, ha, I won't. Don't worry. I'm gonna be in a circus. Ha, ha."

Maybe I am somewhat of a rascal, at that. Maybe. But horses are fun - and smart, too.

WINTER STUFF - AND I'M A YEAR OLDER

There's a lot of stuff going on in the winter on a dairy farm. I help where I can, but barn cleaning is heavy work, so I leave that to the big boys for the time.

I do a good job chasing the cows when we let them out for water. Pa doesn't want them out too long as they can catch cold and won't give as much milk. Ya see, we have a round watering tank outside that has an under-water wood heater to keep the water from freezing. We keep it covered, but open it twice a day for watering.

What I like about winter is it's time to fill the icehouse from the river. The big boys hitch a team of strong horses to the bobsled. It has wooden runners and can hold a heavy load.

Irvin chops a hole in the river, then saws with big wide teeth are used to cut out large squares of ice. Big Irvin manhandles those blocks with ice tongs as if they were made of feathers. He's big and strong, like an ox, that man. The bobsled is loaded, then the big ice cubes are hauled home to our ice house.

I sometimes tie the toboggan behind the sled and ride back and forth to the river. Irvin's fun to be with when he's in a good mood.

I'm fit to be tied! My big excitement comes in February, my birthday, and I'm a whole year older. There'll be more respect now, I'm thinkin'.

SNOW AND WINTER FUN GALORE

There are no great hills to cheer about on the prairie - it's flat as a pancake. But when the winter winds howl during the great prairie blizzards, mountains of snow rise behind trees and buildings. Plenty of hills to slide on, so we farm kids have tons of fun when the chore's are done.

The snow bank on the north side of our house is always as high as my upstairs bedroom window, to give ya an idea of its size. We kids cut steps up one side with a shovel, and then we carry pails of water on top to ice the hill. Sufferin' cats, it's fun.

Heidi, my youngest sister, is a few years older than me. Usually she's happy playin' the piano and messin' with her dolls and stuff, but when there's a lot of snow to play in, she becomes a real buddy to me.

"O.K. Georgie," she says daring me, "let's go whizzing down that hill."

"I'm ready!" I answer excitedly; and away we go flyin' down that hill like the prairie wind.

Heidi has the funniest giggle, and she giggles a lot when she's flyin' lickety split downhill.

When we get all-in from climbing back up the hill, Heidi always comes up with other ideas. After all she's a few years older and I respect her age. Ma always said I must respect my elders.

"Let's build a fort and get ready for a snowball fight", Heidi says. Well, we fight pretty evenly, we two, but when big brother Gordo enters the battle, we younger ones have to join forces. Even so, Gordo has a big advantage; the big moose that he is, so we grudgingly admit defeat.

Sometimes I try some of the older kid-stuff, like trailing a horse with a long rope on skiis. Ma gets worried when she sees some of our antics. Gordo got pretty banged up when he tried skiing behind the Model T Ford and hit a patch of ice, messing up his face for awhile.

We have family fun, too. Pa hitches old Dobbin to the sleigh, away we go. 'Sleigh bells ringin' and the gang all singin' down the road on a moonlit night. Music is a strong part of our family, and we know a lot of tunes to harmonize to; Christmas carols and Stephen Foster ballads are our favorites.

We finished making another freezer full of rich ice cream, and after our sleigh ride we'll settle in on some serious eating of the best ice cream man has ever created. Of course, we'll top it off with a great big spoon of Ma's delicious strawberry preserves.

A STRUGGLE TO MAKE THE GRADE

Will I ever be a real farmer, I wonder? It's sure disgusting that I can't milk cows like the others. Gordo and Irvin won't teach me. They brush me off with such insults as, "Georgie, you're not even dry behind your ears yet." (As if that had anything to do with it). "You hold the cow's tail so it doesn't hit my face when she switches flies," Irvin says. Oh, boy, how insulting can they be, these guys. Holding tails isn't really what I call a great job.

I've got my eyes on those two small cows Pa calls Jersey's. They're light, yellow-brown like a fawn deer color. They'd be a good size for me to start on, I think. Pa says they're "dried up", and they're going to have calves, then, if I'm ready, they'll need to be milked like all the big black and white ones. They're named Bessie and Suzie.

Ya gotta have strong hands to get milk outa' cows spigots, Pa keeps tellin' me. I watch when he milks Flora, the prize cow with a great big bag under her. The boys named Flora for a big neighbor lady, but for the life of me, I don't know why. Those guys are so rambunctious!

Pa tries every trick in the world.

"Here, Georgie," he says, "watch this". Then he squirts milk at the cat sittin' over by the wall.

"Meow", she says, licks herself and stands on her hind legs, waitin' for more. I keep tryin' every chance

I get. I'm so anxious that I keep squeezin' a small rubber ball in my hands to strengthen my fingers.

Finally, success! I do it!

"Ha ha," Pa laughs, "Puddin Head, you'll be a man before your mother yet" he shouts. (He's funny, my Pa).

This very night I wake up hearing an awful commotion downstairs when Pa comes from his nightly barn visit. "We've got twin baby Jersey calves, Georgie! Get up, boy, ya gotta come."

They are two of the cutest little calves I ever did see, I tell ya. Smaller than a baby deer even. I won't be able to milk Bessy and Suzzie for a few weeks, Pa says. The little ones will need all their mommies milk for awhile.

But now I can look forward to two things - teaching the calves to drink from a pail, and soon I'll be able to milk cows like the big boys. I'm so excited, I can't even get to sleep, by golly. I'm feeling more important and getting to be more of a man every day, it seems.

MY INDIAN NEIGHBORS

An exciting part of my life is that Pa has a hayfield close to the Indian School and I get to know Indian kids pretty good. It's fun delivering milk to the school every day, too.

I always feel bad seeing the kids marching in line like tin soldiers, as if they had no feelings. I swear - every day it make me sick to see that. Most town kids are warned to stay away from them. Told they'll catch bad diseases, or something.

I say that's a lot of "horsefeathers!" The real sad thing is that they're so alone and have no playtime. They're plain prisoners - like in jail, I think.

First day taken from reservation mothers. The tots are lined up to get hair cut off.

They're not fenced in, exactly, but white teachers are here to make them tow the mark. They're punished for speaking their own language, or chanting old family songs. Indian ways have to go, white bosses say. I don't understand it, at all.

But being little, I'm curious, and get to know a few kids in time. They're afraid of me as well, but after becoming friends, I lose that fear and hate I was told to show against Indians. It's sickening to see how lonely and sad they look. No laughing, no singing. They're like "whipped puppies."

Then, a strange thing happens. A new teacher moves into one of the school cabins. She becomes a milk customer of ours. Her name is Miss Horne. Jiminy Crickets, she's the prettiest Indian lady I'd every seen - happy, peppy, full of fun.

My brothers call her the "Princess." The town folks are all buzzin' over the beautiful new Indian teacher. Boy, it's like a tornado hit town!

Miss Horne is kind to me and offers me cookies the very first day. She calls me Georgie right away, and that makes me proud. "Georgie," she says while petting Dick, "I was a farm girl and had a horse of my own once. This is sure a fine animal, Georgie."

She's the first Indian teacher - and altogether different - friendly. She's kind to the children, and stands her ground to the old white grouches. With the town behind her like they are, she doesn't back down from her superintendent. She insists the little tykes be allowed to have their Indian customs back; their dances and all. The tots come alive like chipmunks on a bright sunny morning. The people take notice and back her when others interfere. I hear her storm at the other teachers when on the milk route; "No more marching for these little tadpoles! No more!" She insists the tykes get back some of their old customs that'd been denied them since being taken from their own mothers.

Very few Indians are allowed at the school, they would hinder the attempts to change the kids, but my Pa has a garden helper named Taka. He's the grandfather to a little Indian girl, Una, and lives in a shack close to the railroad coal docks. He followed his grandchild here to keep his family from being totally torn apart while Una's at white man's school, he said.

I am lucky to become friends with "Chief Taka," as he is called; and Una becomes a fun playmate for me.

But, without Miss Horne coming to change the rules, I'd probably never have good Indian friends like Una, and her grandfather, Chief Taka.

My Pa grows a big vegetable garden and a stand of tree seedlings. The men are all too busy with farmin' so it was a godsend when Chief Taka offered to do some garden hoeing'.

When I get away from Pa and the boys, I hightail it for the gardens. I could sit and listen to the Chief's stories by the hour. He talks about buffalo hunts with his tribe and many of his good times.

I feel bad when he tells me of the many friends and family he lost trying to survive in his old life.

His eyes water when he tells of losing his woman, and his girl and a son in the battle of Wounded Knee, where his people didn't fire a shot.

He doesn't sound angry. Only sad and lonely for missing his family.

A DEMON HAUNTS US ON THE PRAIRIE

Every morning when I deliver milk, the big Dahlgrin boys always bug me. They sneak around the corner. "Boo!" they shout. "We're gonna git ya Georgie." That kinda stuff always happens to me, but soon I get tough and pay no attention to such bullies.

Don't let anybody tell ya strange things don't go on-on the prairie though.

A most mysterious, devilish intruder invades our neighborhood, and people are frightened out of their wits.

"Georgie, my boy, don't even go out in the dark alone," Ma warns me. "Evil spirit's come to haunt us."

Most prairie folks are church goin', and have no time for the devil. The preacher warns, he's behind every rock. He, too, had a brush with Satan and admits he ran like a scared rabbit.

It's always at night. No one ever sees it - only hears the creature shouting curses and threats of murder! Big men stand guard with guns, but fear drives them home, shaking in their boots.

I might be little, but I think people are being silly. I figured I'd check this thing out for myself one night, so I leave my window open a crack. "Ooooo", the frightful sound: "I'll kill you Georgie!" - I'm sure it said that. Then, it repeats the threat. Goose bumps shoot up my arms - and my hair stands on end! Then, that high screeching, cackling laugh sends icy shivers through me. Oh, Heaven forbid, such evil spirits among us.

Now, the women are getting angry at their cowardly husbands. Besides, they're fed-up over the clotheslines being vandalized nightly. Every bit of clothes hung out to dry is found in a heap next morning. Every clothespin strangely disappears!

Finally, this frosty and hazy night when the moon seems strangely pale, the men folk gather at the river woods. It's been noticed that the pranksters Dahlgrin boys are always sneaking around where the ghostly voices seem most evident. The long-haired goons are usually in some pesky trouble.

Sure enough. The watchmen see the three snickering, lanky boys, enter the woods carrying a wooden cage. Soon, hark! The evil raspy voice echoes from above. "Curses! Curses! Squawk! I'll kill you! I'll kill you!" it shrieks. The watchmen scatter.

Next day, the Constable and men go to the Dahlgrin shack to confront the boys, and demand an explanation.

Well, my friends, the rascals are caught red-handed; clothespins clipped to very possible hanger or curtain.

The boys admit instigating the hoax by using their tame crow to terrorize people. The prank was contrived by splitting the big bird's tongue, they say, and then, they taught him to talk. Every night terrifying the weak of heart - only to have a little fun, they say.

It's a great story for the county newspaper, and the townsfolk all give an embarrassed grin by being taken-in by the Dahlgrin buffoons.

And - the good people that heard the demon will forever give a frightened glance over their shoulder, though, as they remember one of the most scary events of their lives on the prairie. So will I.

MAKIN' HAY WITH HORSES

I'm seven years old now, and a great help at hayin' time. Boy, I'm feeling pretty grown-up for sure.

Pa uses two horses to pull the mower, which cuts a strip of prairie grass about 5 feet wide. It takes a long time to go around 40 acres, so he divides the field in 4 parts. It takes two days to cut; a short time for dryin', and then, Pa says, "C'mom Georgie, it's time for you to get started rakin' hay".

We have one horse, usually Dan my ridin' pal, pull the hay-rake with me on it. I have to dump the hay when the big tines under me get full, and kick the trip lever with my foot when that happens. It's very important that I dump each load next to where I dumped it last time so it lays in long rows. By golly, it means I gotta be on my toes, I tell ya. When that's done, I then steer Dan down the rows and rake the hay into big piles.

I sing a lot when I work. Ya know, since we got that new fangled radio, we're gettin' pretty darn classy out on the prairie, for sure. We hear the New York Opry and everything. That's where I learned "O Sol Mio". My brothers and I see who can out-beller each other. The prairie dogs stand up and seem to applaud, sometimes.

Next, Pa and the big boys "buck" the hay. What that means is they gather the piles I made into bigger piles on wooden planks pulled by two horses. They take that to the center where one great hay-stack is made. I gotta give 'em credit, they're good at that - and - at least it keeps 'em off my back for awhile.

Sometimes when big storms come up I get pretty shaky, especially with thunder and lightenin' crashing all around me. I want to quit and head for cover many times, but Pa won't allow it. He's a great weatherman, my Pa. When it's time to high-tail it for the barn, nearly a mile away, Pa'll put two fingers from each hand in his mouth, and "sufferin' cats", ya can hear that across half the county. Me and the boys all dash for home, get the horses in the barn just as the sky opens up with wind and hail just in the nick of time.

Remember, I said our hay land was next to the Indian School. Well, since Essie Horne came and helped free the kids, I'm happy to see they're allowed to play in the prairie grass hayfield. Buffalo grass it is called by the natives; the grass that fed the millions of buffalo on the prairie before we began to plow it up for other things. Indians worship the land and buffalo which gave them food, as well as the hide for clothing and tepee shelters. Their very existence depended on the land and the great numbers of buffalo. It was after pleasure hunters came and killed the great animals - like squirrels, that the Indian lost his ability to survive his natural way, I soon learned.

Una's grandfather, Taka, praises my Pa for not plowing up that hay land, as there is very little native grass to be found anywhere anymore.

Well, anyway, it's fun to see the school kids when we're in the hay field. They love their Mother Earth, they call it; part of their "Great Spirit". They get a kick out of watching the prairie dogs play on one of the last prairie dog towns in the territory.

We don't stack all the hay. We haul many full loads home to put in the haymow - the upstairs of the barn, above the cows. We'll feed that to the animals when winter comes. Remember, that's when me, Georgie, likes to be in the warm barn with the calves and kitties.

We have other hay fields, too. One alfalfa field is down in the rich river bottom. Cows give more milk if fed alfalfa hay, Pa says.

Now, I told about how cold it gets on the plains in wintertime. Well, that flat land gets as hot as the desert in July, too. Heat of over 100 is common. Now, big brother, Gordo, and I are down in that hollow river bottom, with narry a hint of a breeze. I'm up on the load packin' the hayrack; Gordo's pitchin'. That river draws all kinds of pests; regular flies, horse flies, the worst, and tons of mosquitoes swarm over us in a black cloud.

Gordo has little respect for me, as he tosses the forkful of that dusty hay right on top of me. I scream at him, but it really does no good. He yells back, "Georgie, we gotta get out of here and get home before they eat us alive. There's only one more shock left, then it's home we go".

Yah, tell that to the horses, I'm thinkin'. Their tails are twistin' like a tornado, and their back legs are pounding the ground with mad force as they try to shake off the swarm of flies buggin' 'em.

Finally, tragedy strikes! The horses break away, turn a sharp corner, tip the whole load over, and get tangled up in a big wire fence.

Well, all I can say is I always thought big brother Gordo was tough, but I never saw a two year old baby bawl like that big guy.

Of course, we're both afraid to go home; Pa wouldn't understand, so we go rescue the horses.

Sufferin' cats, we're exhausted; sweat running off in streams, but we have to do it all over again.

MY RABBITS GOTTA GO

I've been worried about this for some time. We had an old empty shed out beyond the cow yard and Pa made a bunch of wire pens to house my pet rabbits. I had more fun caring for my livestock than ya could imagine. I gave them all names and played with each one every day when they were little. I fed 'em alfalfa hay, garden stuff, fresh water, and I cleaned their pens regularly.

It seemed like only a few weeks had passed and I noticed some fur in the opening of the wooden compartment, and thought that was clever of them to pull their own hair out for a warm comfortable bed. It seemed like just a few days later when I went to care for 'em that I had the shock of my life. I could see in that nest squirming little critters; baby rabbits! Wow!

Eventually, Pa was building more pens. Looking back on it, seemed like Pa spent a lot of time buildin' pens. I kept naming my wonderful pets, and enjoyed caring for them.

I suppose a year had gone by when Pa started putting pens on the opposite wall, and we began talking about what on earth we were going to do about the big number of Chinchilla Rabbits.

My friends, I'm two years older now than when Pa started me out on my livestock project, and I hope you'll understand that I'm not a mean fella when I agreed with Pa that we had to do something radical to end this problem.

So, what's happening here is that I'm sitting in my rabbit shed trying to explain to a bunch of lovable fuzzballs that I can't take care of 'em anymore. I don't suppose they understand.

But, I've got a problem with turning 'em over to Dump-ground Scotty. Scotty's kind of a hermit who lives in a little square shack out of junk people threw away, and furnished it the same way. At first, I was happy to turn my prize rabbits over to Scotty, but after I heard him drool over the amount of meat on these lovable pets of mine, I had some misgivings.

I decided I had to do somethin' rash. I fibbed a bit when tellin' the folks I had a bit of a headache and didn't want to go to the church social tonight. I was determined to free my buddies. I set up a master plan.

As soon as Ma and Pa pulled out of the yard in their horseless buggy, I hurried to the barn and threw a harness on old Dan, hooked him to the two-wheeled cart and loaded up most of the pens for the big escape. I had a lump in my throat and was might afraid, should I get caught.

I take those lucky rabbits down to the alfalfa patch by the river - plenty of their favorite food and water for them to live on - and I let them have their freedom. Plenty of old hollow logs to seek shelter in. I am sure they'll be fine.

It won't be easy to tell Pa, "Holy moly, I sure must 'av left the door of the rabbit shack open by mistake". But, I leave a few behind - Big Boy, Johnny, Suzzy, and Flicker - who seem content to stay by the shack.

As tame as those buddies are, I know they'll be beggin' to be petted from time to time, even while free.

So, anyway, like I've been taught, it's okay once in awhile to tell a little white lie if it's to protect someone from pain, or danger. And, I think this was a worthwhile rescue mission.

I kinda hide the wetted eyes I can't hold back over losing my fine pets. But, I'm older now and realize I have to concentrate on more demanding needs of our farm animals and the other farm work beggin' my attention. Well, anyway, I guess bunnies are really for little kids.

HURRAY! IT'S THRESHING TIME

Pa makes the old Fordson tractor huff and puff, as the long power belt chugs and churns the threshing machine! "Heave ho, heave ho!", he shouts out. And a whole bunch a farm hands begin workin' together like bees in a beehive harvestin' the grain. "Golden Grain" - it's the reward farmers get for a hard summer's work.

Me? I got my important job too. As the grain drops down into the wagon box it's my job to move the spout back and forth so the grain gets spread out evenly and won't clog in the pipe. Pa would certainly rap me hard on the backside if I let that happen. The old crew boss won't stand for any foolishness, for sure.

That big old threshing machine is like magic for what it does. Ya' see, we've got a crew of about 15 hands all doing important work to keep things hummin' the way Pa wants.

It takes 10 teams and 10 hayracks with about 12 guys pitching bundles to keep that hungry thresher goin'. As soon as the first two men are done feeding the machine, they hightail it to the field like beavers for another load. Threshing is fun, even though it's hard work. The men laugh and sing over the noisy machine as it whacks and shakes the grain off the stems of the bundles. The long main spout on the opposite end shoots out those stems and soon a great straw pile grows as the day continues.

I think I told you that our farm was right by town, so, like a circus, the town folks gather around to see the fun. When things are goin' good, my Pa likes to entertain, and sometimes he even does a little jig. When things aren't good, watch out! Pa turns into a bit of a tiger. Well, not exactly.

I like to show off how I can work. I flex my muscles to Una and Gramps Taka when they come in from the tree patch to take in the excitement. Una laughs and says, "You're funny, Georgie". Then she kicks off her shoes, climbs on the wheel and jumps in the grain and half buries herself. I get a kick outa' her. She's fulla' fun. Pa likes having Taka and Una around too.

A lot of things happen to upset routine though, like one of the guys feeding the bundles tosses in too many and jams the big machine. My Pa, good churchman that he is, shouts in angry Swedish. It's good no one understands him, maybe.

Suddenly a big black horse standing next to the rig gets his tail caught in one of those flywheels, or whatever. What a spectacle! The horse takes off, leaving half of his tail hair behind. The driver bounces off the back when the team stampedes away.

The townspeople cheer thinking its part of the event. The horse, when caught, looks a bit embarrassed with only a half tail, though.

It's really fun when these old boys and the young ones, too, break for lunch. A big hungry threshing crew doesn't stand on refinement. They dig in like

31

hungry wolves at the table. It's laughable to see those jokers pitch food in their mouths as fast as they feed the threshing machine.

Ma has a lot of help, too. Neighbor ladies come to fix a dozen or more chickens, tons of potatoes, beans, corn, and what not. There's always 3 or 4 kinds of pie and some guys have to try 'em all. Ma won't complain as long as they eat what she cooks.

I'm just a little bit peeved though. Why can't I sit at the big long table like the rest of the crew? They put me off in the kitchen on a stool with the women. It's disgusting being treated so shabby like, I think.

Ma makes me feel good, though, when she says, "Georgie, would you like to take this plate of chicken and a few pieces of pie out to Taka and Una?" I'm happy Ma remembered them.

ALL'S DONE BUT THE SHOUTIN'

Well, friends, I'm glad you joined me for a good time on the prairie farm as we milked the cows, fed the chickens, put up hay, threshed the grain and everything. We've almost gone full circle, as they say, doin' all the things there's to be done on a dairy farm.

Don't forget Pa's big garden Chief Taka and little Una cared for all summer. Well, Taka has gone back to his roots on the reservation for a while, and Una is back in school for another winter. I'll wave at her every day we meet at the Indian School when I deliver milk in our new Model T Ford milk wagon. It's not as romantic as Dick, The Buckskin Wonder Horse was, but we can go a little faster, so I'll get to school on time every day now.

Meanwhile, back here on the farm, though, we've got plenty to do before the snow flies again. Pa has a great big root cellar under the porch at one end of our basement, and we've got a lot of veggies to store for the winter. Pa plants lots of squash, potatoes, carrots, and stuff that'll be good eating when it turns cold. So, I'm busy with the rest, pickin' up lots of garden stuff.

Ma's been no piker, either. She and the girls have been cannin' up a storm. I'll bet she's got 500 quarts of canned tomatoes, corn, beans, and all. They'll be great when the winter storms keep us home, and we'll all be entertained with the new wonderful radio we got on the prairie this year.

Pa's a little worried. He looks up at the sky quite a bit, bein' the great weatherman people give him credit for and says, "We've had a few dry weeks and the winds have kicked up some big dust storms. Maybe what Chief Taka says about tearin' up too much of the skin of the earth will come back to haunt us on the prairie". Time will tell, I suppose.

Our farm is set in the valley of rich soil, so we'll probably always have good farming. But some of my folks friends up on the sandy highlands have already "thrown in the towel", sold their goods and have taken off for California with their old open touring cars.

So, my life has been hunky dory. I work hard, like the rest of the family, but I enjoy all the wonderful animals around me all the time.

I hope you've enjoyed your visit as we worked and played on our prairie dairy farm. Thank ya' for comin'. I sure enjoyed havin' ya'.

Georgie

TRIVIA OF THE TIME

THE ROARING TWENTIES

They called it "The Roaring Twenties" - and roaring it was. From a rather silent world, only interrupted by the clippety-clop of occasional horses hooves and the sound of isolated thunderclaps, the air was suddenly filled with a constant buzz. This noise was created by a multitude of horseless carriages, a result of Henry Ford's Folly of mass producing the old Model T in various forms and stiles: one seaters, two seaters - take your pick. Just about everybody could afford one, if he could come up with just a few hundred dollars - the going price. The repair kit required was merely a hammer, pliers and a piece of bailing wire. Of course, there were some "well-heeled cats" like the banker and the "honest town lawyer" who sported big limousines - Stutz Bearcats, and twelve cylinder Hudsons, and like that. But there were a very few folks in that category, so just about everybody else had Ford coups, or roadsters, or covered touring rigs. I tell you, it was an amazing spin the country was on.

People were taking more chances now they had wheels to roam around in. We used to spy on the early "swingers". That pompous rascal dentist was extra appreciative of the great work his secretary did for him, obviously, so he gave her numerous rides down cherry lane out to our hayland quite frequently. We farm boys weren't above doing a little spyin' for causal entertainment.

THEN THERE WAS MUSIC

The only extra-curricular sound filling our house was the snoring of Ma and the coughing of Pa, who'd been out behind the barn again -smoking. Oh, my, how he preached us kids about the evils of smoking. Oh, well. But now, they figured out how to send music and talking through the air. Will wonders never cease, we thought. Pa got a big console radio for the home. Trouble is, Pa wanted that baritone gospel singer from Texas on always and we kids wanted to listen to one of the "big bands" flooding the country. Swing and Sway with Sammy Kay, Little Jack Little, Tommy and Jimmy

Dorsey, Tex Benikey, The Snickafritz Band - you name it, we could tell them all by their distinctive theme music.

Thank goodness, radios became as prevalent as hen's eggs. Even Mother's Oats came up with a great promotion. A free crystal radio with every purchase. Well, it was fun out on the prairie dreaming about dancing to Russ Morgan at the Treanon Ball Room in Chicago. One day...one day, maybe we'd be able to go to Chicago, or New York, or wherever a particular radio broadcast emanated from.

My Lord in Heaven, it was an excitin' time to be alive in this world.

THEN THERE WAS THAT CROW WE TALKED ABOUT

Talk to any bird authority and you'll find out I'm not just joshing about their ability to talk. The big problem with crows is they're too darn smart to catch. You know, they move only far enough from the road to keep beyond the wheels. That's smart. Haw many dead crows have you seen on the roadway? Narry a one.

ESTHER HORNE HONORED BY COUNTY HISTORICAL FOLKS

Esther Horne was the most impressionable person I've known. We exchanged books, talked on telephone, sent greetings, and tried to arrange a meeting. I hadn't seen her for seventy years. After arranging to meet at Naytahwaush Reservation in May 1999, she related by phone that I should come a day earlier than planned - she was not well. For some reason it was not possible for me to go, but when I finally arrived there, I found her lake cabin vacated. I learned from her neighbors that she had been taken in emergency, to the Wahpeton, N.D. hospital.

I now want to pay tribute to her by including the written program presented by her County Historical Society.

ESTHER BURNETT HORNE

The great-great granddaughter of Sacajawea,
Shoshone girl guide of the Lewis and Clark Expedition.

Mrs. Horne is an enrolled member of the Wind River Shoshone Tribe of Indians in Fort Washakie, Wyoming. She has contributed her bit of history by researching, writing and lecturing on Native American Oral and Written History. She has published a monograph on the *"Oral Tradition of Sacajawea"*.

Mrs. Horne retired in 1965 after an eminent career of over 30 years as an elementary and demonstration teacher with the Bureau of Indian Affairs and received its highest honor, the Distinguished Service Award. Her career has been one of singular leadership and noteworthy contributions. She has enriched the academic, social, and cultural needs of hundreds of Indian and non-Indian children and adults.

Organization and Civic Activity: She organized the first Girl Scout Troop in Wahpeton and the first Indian Girl Scout Troop in the U.S. and worked actively with scouts throughout her career. Her emphasis was the virtue of Indian culture by teaching Indian values, costume construction, authentic Indian dances, the contributions of Indians to civilization, and other aspects of Indian history. The beautiful interpretation of the 23rd Psalm, in Indian Sign Language by her students, has become widely known. She wrote and directed 3 historical pageants: *"Buckskin to Broadcloth"*, *"Prairie Rama of the Red River Valley"* and *"North Dakota, The Heart of the Continent"*. She was the inspiration for the Chippewa Indian decor in the Samuel Memorial Episcopal Church in Naytahwaush, MN. She has written many articles on Indian Culture and Education published in School Arts Magazine, Child Life, American Girl, My Weekly Reader, Indian Education and in various state and national news media. Esther and her husband assisted many disadvantaged Indian children by taking them into their home. She continues her role as a consultant on Indian education and history as an Indian resource person for teaching methods of self esteem and pride in heritage.

Esther is included in:
* First comprehensive directory of American Indian / Alaska Native Women as Educational and Native American Oral History Consultant
* Indian Council Fire: National Congress of American Indians
* Guide of Lewis and Clark Sesquicentennial Expeditions
* North Dakota Federated Women's Club
* White House Conference on Children and Youth Delegate
* Good Will Ambassador to nine European Countries to promote travel and sale of Indian Arts and Crafts of the Midwest for ND and the U. S. Travel Bureaus
* Girls Scouts of the U.S.A. 30 years
* Consultant on Indian Affairs at large and continues as a public speaker and consultant on Native America.

Esther's honors include:
* Who's Who in North Dakota
* Outstanding Teacher Award
* First Master Teacher in Bureau of Indian Affairs
* Sertoma Clubs Woman of the Year in Bismarck, ND
* Distinguished Service Award in Education from the Department of the Interior
* Model for Sacajawea bust for State Historical Society of ND, Bismarck
* Recipient of Jefferson Peace Medal from Lewis and Clark Sesquicentennial Committee
* 1997 Honored Woman by Episcopal Women, in the MN Diocese.

Esther was married to Robert Horne (Hoopa) of California (deceased.) Children: Yvonne (Bill) Barney, (deceased); Dianne (Everett) Kjelbertson, Naytahwaush, three grand-children, three great-grandchildren.

As the Bicentennial of the Lewis and Clark expedition draws closer and we take note of the many activities being considered in celebration of the event, we recognize with pride the many contributions to American History made by its members.

Of special historical importance to our nation were the special activities of the Shoshone Indian girl guide, Sacajawea. (Mrs. Horne's great-great grandmother.) Her keen judgment, quick wit and know-ledge made it possible to secure horses from other tribes, obtain food and medicines from plants along the way, and save many valuable papers when boats capsized.   She was a role model for her descendants and women in general.

. . . .

Be sure to stop and view the many beautiful and historical artifacts on the main floor, which have been donated by The Horne Family.

Other V.G. Hedner books:

<u>THE BIG SWEDE</u>

"The Big Swede" is an epic saga of Olaf Olsson, who survives a Baltic shipwreck and pursues his dream to America in 1850.

Excitement abounds as Olaf, a giant of a man, master horseman and wagoner, blazes trails from Prairie du Chien to Canada. Known for brute strength, yet, he is a kind and gentle man.

His heart flutters when he falls for a pretty Métis maiden. First he must win over her pledge to a saintly commitment.

With his great horse, Olaf continues his legendary heroics: An expert rifleman, he is often challenged - never defeated.

True to a vow to his Métis in holy seclusion, the tall blond Swede is admired by many beauties: Temptation plagues him.

He fishes with Taoyateduta (Little Crow), Sioux chief. They have a strong friendship, but, when the tribe goes hungry, the hostile braves see Olaf as only a "white" man.

After years, the lovers meet by chance. There is much hurt, but renewed faith rekindles the flame. Will love prevail?

Forced to starvation the angered renegade Indians revolt and murder German farmers-like sheep! The prairie burns! Olaf defends innocent refugees at Fort Ridgely as flaming arrows rain on the Fort and towns. A thousand will die!

After two months, a large government army defeats the Sioux. Hostiles escape to the Dakota Territory. Revenge is dealt to the friendly Indians. Thirty eight are hanged en masse.

Will Olaf's future take a positive turn? Will the sun shine on his dreams again? One must read "The Big Swede" to find if all ends well in this action filled epic saga.

ORDER FORM

Mail to: Castle Marketing
             Vicksburg Plaza, Suite 4
             1115 Vicksburg Lane
             Plymouth, MN 55447

Your name: _____

Street: _____

City: _____State/Zip: _____

Indicate the book you wish to order below:
****

"The Big Swede" Historical novel ISBN 0-9661383-1-7
420 pages. Indicate your selection below.

_____ Hard cover $19.95

_____ Soft cover $15.95

$ 1.75   Please include $1.75 for shipping costs.

_____ Total
****

"Georgie Farm Boy of the Prairie" ISBN 0-9661383-3-3

_____ Soft cover $8.95

$ 1.05   Please include $1.05 for shipping costs.

_____Total

Books will be mailed within 24 hours after receiving the
order. Telephone orders will get immediate action. Call 952-
476-0685 Wayzata, MN for the fastest results. We will bill
you.